MARGRET & H. A. REY's

Curious George

Visits a Toy Shop

WALKER BOOKS
AND SUBSIDIARIES

LONDON · BOSTON · SYDNEY · AUCKLAND

First published in Great Britain 2006
by Walker Books Ltd, 87 Vauxhall Walk, London SE11 5HJ

6 8 10 9 7

© 2002 Houghton Mifflin Company
Curious George® is a registered trademark of Houghton Mifflin Company
Published by arrangement with Houghton Mifflin Company

This book has been typeset in Gill Sans MT Schoolbook
Illustrated in the style of H. A. Rey by Martha Weston

Printed in China

British Library Cataloguing in Publication Data:
a catalogue record for this book is available from the British Library

ISBN 978-0-7445-7050-2

www.walker.co.uk

This is George.

He was a good little monkey and always very curious.

Today was the opening of a brand-new toy shop. George
and the man with the yellow hat did not want to be late.

When they arrived, the queue to go inside wound all the way around the corner. When a queue is this long, it's not easy for a little monkey to be patient.

George sneaked through the crowd.

All he wanted was a peek inside.

George got to the door just as the owner opened it.

"This is no place for a monkey," she said.

But George was so excited he was already inside!

Balls, dolls, bicycles and games filled the shelves.

There were so many toys.

George didn't even know

how some of them worked.

And how about these hoops?

What did they do?

George was curious.

He climbed up to pull

one out of the pile.

It would not move.

George pulled harder.

Still it wouldn't move.

George pulled with all fours.

Suddenly there was a terrible crash. Red, blue, green
and yellow hoops bounced up and down and everywhere.
"Look!" exclaimed a boy, bouncing up and down himself.
"Why, I haven't seen one of these in years!"
said the boy's grandmother.

She put a hoop around her waist and gave it a spin.

George tried the hula hoop, too!

Then George pretended to be a wheel.

He rolled and rolled and...

Oops! He rolled right into the owner.
The owner shook her head.
"I knew you were trouble,"
she said. "Now you've made
a mess of my new shop."

Again she tried to stop George.

And again George was too quick.

In only a second he was around the corner and onto the highest shelf.

Below him, George saw a
little girl point to a toy out of
reach. "Mummy, can we get that dinosaur?" she asked.

George picked up the dinosaur
and lowered it to the girl.
She was delighted. So was the
small boy next to her.

"Could you get that ball for me,
please?" he asked George.
George reached up, grabbed the
ball, and bounced it to the boy.

"May I have that puppet, way over there?" asked another girl.